OUTSIDE AND INSIDE
KANGAROOS

BY SANDRA MARKLE

ATHENEUM BOOKS FOR YOUNG READERS

For Meredith Gould, who is a bright new light in our family

The author would like to especially thank Professor Ken Richardson, Division of Veterinary and Biomedical Science, Murdoch University, Australia, for sharing his expertise and enthusiasm. Thanks also to J. Louis Harris, D.V.M. of Tucker, Georgia.

ATHENEUM BOOKS FOR YOUNG READERS
An imprint of Simon & Schuster Children's Publishing Division
1230 Avenue of the Americas
New York, New York 10020
Text copyright © 1999 by Sandra Markle
The text of this book is set in Melior.
Printed in Hong Kong
10 9 8 7 6 5 4 3 2
Library of Congress Cataloging-in-Publication Data
Markle, Sandra.
Outside and Inside Kangaroos / by Sandra Markle.—1st ed.
p.   cm.
Summary: Describes the inner and outer workings of kangaroos,
including their diet, anatomy, and life cycle.
ISBN 0-689-81456-9
1. Kangaroos—Juvenile literature. [1. Kangaroos.] I. Title.
QL737.M35M272   1999
599.2'2—DC21
98-45354

NOTE: To help readers pronounce words that may not be familiar to them, pronunciations are given in the glossary/index. Glossary words are italicized the first time they appear.

TITLE PAGE: Group drinking together

AUSTRALIA

NEW ZEALAND

Kangaroos are some of Earth's most unusual animals. They live only in Australia and a few nearby places. What makes kangaroos so unusual? For one thing, some of them are the biggest *marsupials,* animals whose babies develop inside a pocketlike pouch. Some kangaroos are also the world's biggest animals that move around by hopping. Think about it. Camels, giraffes, elephants, hippos, rhinos—only kangaroos are hoppers.

Look at the red kangaroo, opposite, and the musky rat kangaroo, below. The red kangaroo is much bigger. In fact, red kangaroos are the largest kind of kangaroo—sometimes as tall as the tallest basketball players. Musky rat kangaroos, on the other hand, are the smallest kind—usually no taller than a two-liter soft drink bottle.

Can you spot ways that the red kangaroo and the musky rat kangaroo are alike? All kangaroos have certain things in common: strong back legs and big hind feet just right for hopping, a big middle toe to help push off in a hop, a tail for balance, no thumb, and, in females, a pouch for their young.

How fast can you hop? Kangaroos have been clocked at speeds over forty-eight kilometers (thirty miles) per hour. Have an adult drive you in an automobile at that speed to get a feel for it. So how do kangaroos hop so fast? And why do they hop?

Studies by Dr. Richard Taylor and others at Duke and Harvard Universities have shown that hopping saves the kangaroo energy. A fast-hopping kangaroo does not breathe harder or use much more energy than a slow-hopping kangaroo. The reason for this is its *tendons*—stretchy bands that connect its legs to its feet.

Feel the ridge on the back of your ankle. That is your tendon, but it is nowhere near as big or as stretchy as a kangaroo's. When a kangaroo's feet strike the ground in a hop, the energy of hitting the ground is stored as the tendons are pressed together. Then, like a bouncing rubber ball, the tendons spring back, pushing the kangaroo into the air again. At full speed, a kangaroo is off the ground most of the time. Its long hind legs fold and unfold so its feet can touch down and spring up again, but its body stays at about the same height. The kangaroo almost seems to glide through the air.

If you could look inside a kangaroo, you would discover what makes the hop work—*bones* and *muscles.* Just as a building has a strong framework to support it and give it shape, a kangaroo's body, like yours, has a framework too—a bony *skeleton.* Now that you can see its skeleton, take a close look at the kangaroo's legs. They are bent while the kangaroo is standing. So to jump, a kangaroo straightens its legs. The small front legs and big tail help keep the upper body from being top-heavy when the kangaroo pushes off in a hop. Next, check out the kangaroo's big feet. You will see that it has four toes. The kangaroo really hops on these toes.

Do you wonder why a kangaroo's skeleton has lots of bones? Its body, like yours, can only bend where two bones meet. Having lots of bones lets it bend and twist easily. As the kangaroo hops, the upper body twists to turn left or right.

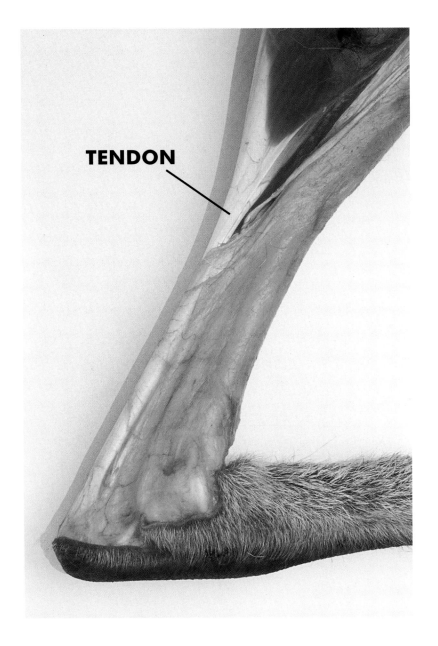

TENDON

Take a look inside a kangaroo's ankle and you'll see the springy tendon—the white band. Where the tendon appears to form a *V,* it attaches to the red leg muscle. Muscles move bones, and a kangaroo's muscles power its hops. In fact, about half of a kangaroo's weight is muscle—almost twice as much as other animals its size.

Crouch with your body bent at the knees and the hip. This is the way a kangaroo's legs are bent while resting. A kangaroo is always ready to hop. To launch the kangaroo into the air, the muscles pull on the leg bones, straightening them. But the muscles can only pull on bones, not push them. So to fold the legs again for another leap, a kangaroo's body, like yours, has pairs of muscles—one to stretch, one to pull back. A big red kangaroo can leap as much as nine meters (twenty-seven feet) in one bound.

A kangaroo's big tail is very useful. You already know it helps the kangaroo balance when hopping. This red kangaroo is leaning on its tail while it scratches what itches. When a kangaroo moves slowly, its tail is even more important because most kinds of kangaroos can't move their two hind feet separately. So to move forward, the kangaroo leans over until its front feet are touching the ground. Next, using its big tail for support, the kangaroo swings its two hind feet ahead of the front legs. Then, it moves the front legs forward again and starts the process over.

The kangaroo's small front feet are handlike and have five toes, though only four show in this photo. None of these toes works like a thumb, though. Try picking up something without using your thumb to check out how a kangaroo's front feet work.

Look at the kangaroo's long, sharp claws. These help the kangaroo hold onto things. The kangaroo also uses its claws to groom its woolly coat. Like a cat, a kangaroo will sometimes lick its front feet and run them over its fur.

Why do you think this red kangaroo is digging a hole?

Did you guess that the kangaroo was digging a hole to stay cool? Red kangaroos live where it is hot and dry. So they are usually active at night and spend the hot daytime hours resting. In open grassland, where there is very little shade, a kangaroo digs a shallow hole to lie in. Being at least partly below the surface shields the kangaroo's body from the heat reflecting off the ground.

When the day heats up, the red kangaroo needs more than a hole to stay cool, so it *pants,* or breathes fast. Air passing rapidly over moist tissue inside its mouth cools off the kangaroo. Drooling helps too.

Red kangaroos have other ways to beat the heat on a really hot day. When you are hot, you *sweat* to cool off. As this moisture evaporates from your skin, some heat energy is used up, making you feel cooler. Living where water is scarce, the red kangaroo's body has adapted to use water sparingly. So red kangaroos only sweat while they are being active. When a kangaroo stops moving, it stops sweating. Then, to cool off, a red kangaroo licks its forearms, spreading *saliva,* the moisture produced in its mouth. This offers the same cooling effect as sweating with less water loss.

You may be surprised that licking such a small area as its forearms could cool off a big kangaroo. This trick works because the kangaroo has a lot of blood vessels just under the skin on its forearms. So the evaporating spit draws heat away from the blood flowing through these blood vessels.

As evening comes and the day cools off, kangaroos start to eat. Adults that live where food is scarce usually have home ranges several kilometers square, but they'll share this range with other kangaroos. A gathering of kangaroos, like these grays, is not really a group, though. At the first sign of danger, kangaroos hop off in all directions, every kangaroo for itself. It's no wonder groups of kangaroos are called *mobs*.

Life for a kangaroo is one big meal—they eat and eat and eat. In fact, kangaroos spend nearly every waking moment eating. They only eat plants, but not every kind of kangaroo eats the same kind of plants. For example, the little musky rat kangaroo eats a variety of plant leaves, fruit, and bark. The red kangaroo, on the other hand, mainly eats grass. In fact, it eats a lot of grass. It takes a lot of food energy for such a big kangaroo to be active and stay healthy. Since ranchers want the grass for their sheep and cattle, they think kangaroos are pests.

A kangaroo's teeth and jaws are designed to make it an eating machine. See the space between the kangaroo's two big bottom teeth? Now feel your lower jaw by grabbing your chin. Your lower jaw is one piece. A kangaroo's lower jaw is two bones joined by a flexible band that lets the two halves move separately. As a kangaroo grabs a mouthful of grass, the lower jaw spreads, making room for a bigger mouthful.

The kangaroo's upper and lower teeth act like scissors, snipping off the plants. At the same time, the kangaroo jerks its head up, helping to snap any stems that are still connected.

Just behind the kangaroo's front teeth, there is a space where the kangaroo's tongue pushes the plants into wads. Next, the big jaws slide side to side, grinding up the plants with special ridged grinding teeth called molars. You have molars too, but they are bumpy, not ridged. Open your mouth wide and look in the mirror to see the big molars in the back of your mouth.

Kangaroos spend hours chewing. Plants contain a lot of a rough material called silica—so much that chewing some grasses can be like chewing sandpaper. In time, enough grinding will wear out a kangaroo's teeth, but don't worry. A kangaroo has replacement teeth. Like a moving checkout counter at a grocery store, the molars slowly slide forward in both the upper and lower jaws. This is timed perfectly so that by the time the grinding surface is worn away, the molar reaches the front of the row and falls out. By then a new molar will have developed in back of the row and moved into place. There is one catch to this tooth-replacement system. Kangaroos only produce about sixteen molars during their lifetime. So a really old kangaroo could run out of teeth.

If you look back at the book's title page, you will see red kangaroos drinking water. Like you, a red kangaroo needs water to live, but it can go several days without drinking. This is possible because the kangaroo eats moist green plants that supply some water. Its body also recycles water so that little is lost when it passes wastes.

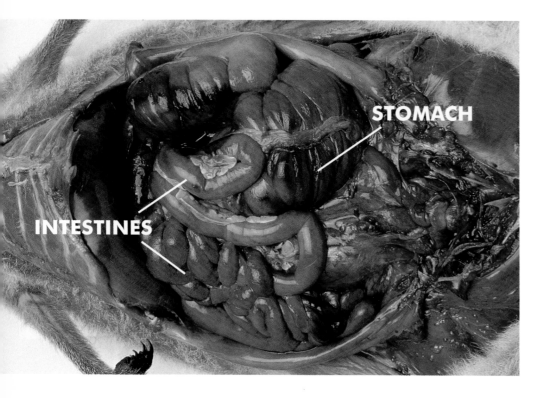

STOMACH

INTESTINES

When you swallow, that's the end of chewing your food, but that's not true for kangaroos. The first part of a kangaroo's digestive system acts like a holding tank. When the kangaroo is resting, it coughs up this food again, one wad at a time. Then the kangaroo chews the plants some more before swallowing again.

Next, the mashed wad of plant material moves into the kangaroo's *stomach*. No matter how well the kangaroo chews its food, it can't break down the cellulose, tough fibers that act like the plant's supporting skeleton. So a kangaroo gets a little help from some tiny living things—*bacteria*. A kangaroo's stomach contains millions of bacteria that eat cellulose. These bacteria digest the plant fibers, producing food *nutrients* in the form of sugar and starch. The bacteria need the sugar and starch to live, but they produce more than they can use, so their wastes contain lots of sugar and starch. These become part of the kangaroo's food supply.

From the stomach, the partly digested food moves into a long, winding tube, the *small intestine.* Some bacteria enter the intestine along with the plant material. Then more digestive juices break down the bacteria and finish breaking down the food into nutrients. The food nutrients pass into the bloodstream and are carried to all parts of the kangaroo's body to help it live and be active.

Finally, the food material moves into the *large intestine.* Here more cellulose-eating bacteria give the kangaroo a second chance to get food nutrients from the plants it ate. What's left after this process is passed out as waste pellets.

STOMACH WITH PARTLY DIGESTED FOOD

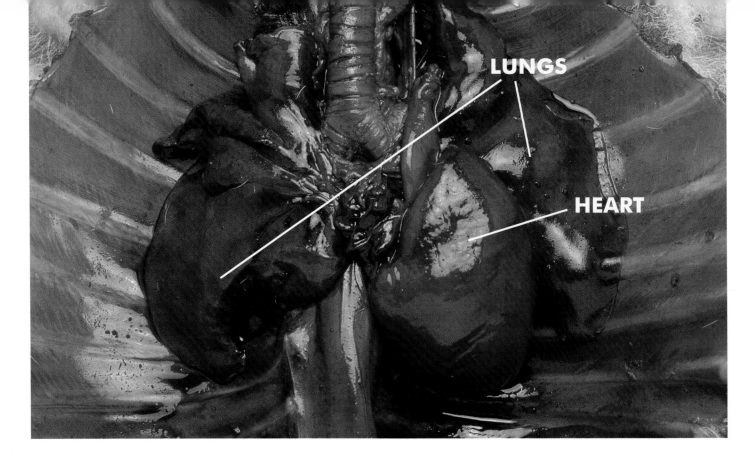

LUNGS

HEART

To make use of food nutrients, a kangaroo needs a steady supply of *oxygen,* one of the gases in the air. Oxygen combines with the food nutrients to release the energy the kangaroo needs to be active, stay warm, and grow. Like you, when a kangaroo breathes in, air flows down the *windpipe* into the *lungs,* where oxygen is exchanged for the waste gas *carbon dioxide.* Then the kangaroo breathes out this waste gas.

The kangaroo's blood carries oxygen and nutrients through its body. The pump that pushes the blood is a special muscle, the *heart.* But a kangaroo does not control its heartbeat the way it does its hops. The heart has a built-in pacemaker that keeps it beating, while the kangaroo's *brain* controls how fast or slow the heart pumps—fast when active, slow when resting.

Did you guess that these two red kangaroo males are fighting? When they fight, the males stand tall, lock their forearms, and wrestle. They throw their heads way back to protect their eyes and ears from being scratched by sharp claws. At any moment, one of the males is likely to rock back on its tail and kick the other. They will keep on punching, wrestling, pawing, and kicking until one male breaks away and retreats.

Why do you think the two males are fighting?

Sometimes male kangaroos will fight over a shady resting place or access to water in hot weather. Usually, though, male kangaroos fight for a mate.

Red kangaroos will mate at any time of year as long as there is plenty of food and water. Whenever kangaroos mate, a *cell* from the male, called a *sperm,* joins with the female's *egg* cell. Then the young, or *embryo,* begins to 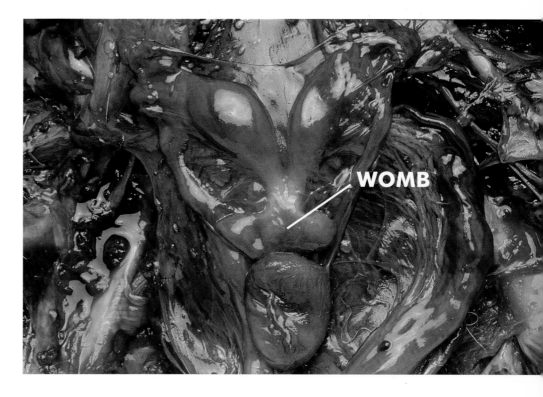 develop inside the mother in a body part called the *womb.*

From the time a female kangaroo is about two years old—old enough to begin to have babies—she is nearly always pregnant. In fact, she will usually have babies in three different stages of development: one in her womb, one inside her pouch, and one at her side. Once the baby leaves the womb and enters the pouch, it is called a *joey.*

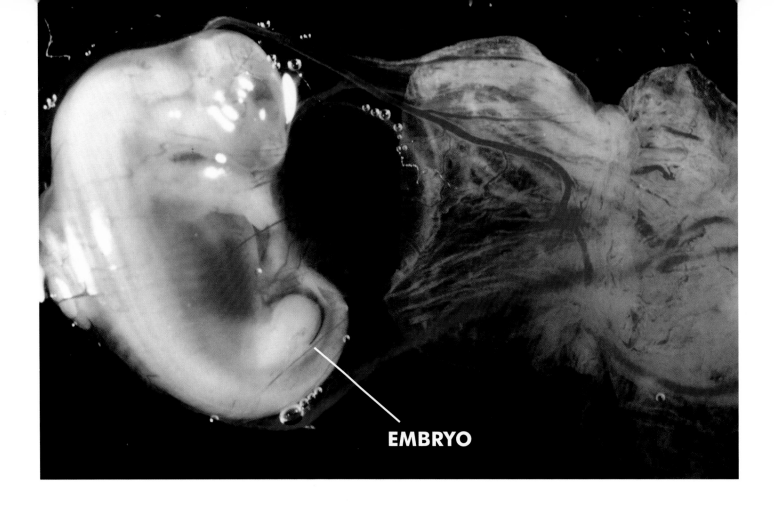

EMBRYO

This is a kangaroo embryo developing inside the womb. Can you see its eyes and ears already beginning to form? Can you spot its heart?

Like you developing inside your mother, the baby is inside a fluid-filled sack with blood vessels connecting to the mother's body. Her body supplies the food nutrients the baby needs to develop and exchanges oxygen for its waste gas, carbon dioxide. In kangaroos, birth, the moment when the embryo leaves the womb, happens after only thirty to forty days. Before you were born, you developed for about 270 days—nine months.

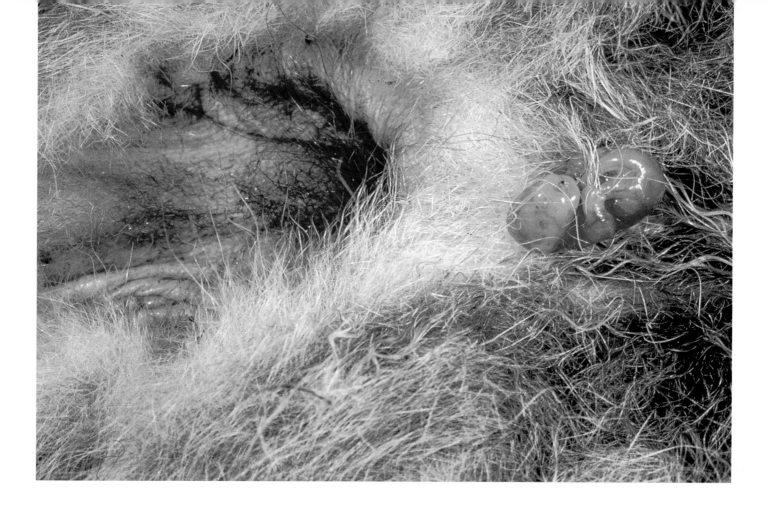

Blind, hairless, and about the size of a bumblebee, this newborn joey is crawling through its mother's fur to the pouch. Its tiny forearms and claws help it hang onto Mom's hair and its sense of smell guides it toward the pouch and the waiting milk supply. The thin cord connecting the baby to its mother has snapped, but its body is not yet fully developed. So the joey has to make it to the warm, safe pouch to survive.

Not every baby kangaroo reaches its mother's pouch, but this one did. Once inside the pouch, the tiny baby takes a nipple into its mouth and begins to suck. The nipple swells to fill the joey's mouth. This helps the baby stay firmly attached inside the pouch while the mother is hopping. This joey has been growing for just three days. It will stay continuously attached to the nipple, suckling for more than 100 days.

This joey is 105 days old. Look how it has changed!

A kangaroo mother's milk supplies all of the food nutrients her baby needs to live and grow. For the first three months, the joey is very small and can only suck a few drops of milk at a time, so it grows very slowly. Once the joey is big enough to suck more milk, the content of the mother's milk changes. Now it contains more *fat* and *protein*—food nutrients needed for growth and tissue development. Then the joey grows rapidly.

Although her body is working to provide for her baby, the mother kangaroo pays little attention to the joey growing inside her pouch. She does keep her baby clean, though, by regularly poking her head into her pouch and licking up the baby's wastes.

After about 120 days of growing, the joey is big enough that a foot or tail may sometimes poke out of the pouch. After another month, the joey has grown a fur coat and can regulate its own body temperature.

This baby gray kangaroo is peeking at the outside world. But it will stay inside the pouch, suckling and growing for another month before it is ready to take its first hop. During this time, mother and baby get to know each other. The mother licks a foot, a tail, a head—whatever part sticks out of her pouch. The joey in turn spends more time with its head poking out. It sniffs Mom and the world. While the mother is grazing, the joey may even reach out to touch the ground or nibble blades of grass.

What in the world could this joey be doing?

Did you guess that the joey is poking its head into its mother's pouch to suckle?

Usually a joey first leaves the pouch by falling out. This often happens with a little help from Mom. A mother kangaroo can contract the muscles that control the size of her pouch and the pouch opening. So, to get her baby out of her pouch and into the world, she just tips her body forward and relaxes the pouch muscles.

On its first outing, the joey is likely to stand up on wobbly legs, look around, and then climb right back into the pouch. From then on, though, it will be in and out of the pouch, but never far from Mom. Dingos, foxes, and eagles can attack baby kangaroos, so Mom stays alert. If she senses danger, she makes a sound to signal her baby and bends forward, holding the pouch wide open. Kicking off with its hind legs, the joey does a complete somersault and enters the pouch, facing the opening. Then, like pulling the strings on a garbage bag, Mom contracts the pouch muscles, sealing the opening. Once the danger is past, she relaxes her muscles and the joey pops its head out once again. As you might guess, the bigger the baby kangaroo grows, the harder it is for the youngster to fit into Mom's pouch. This baby is so big it can only poke its head in.

This isn't a kangaroo kiss. The young red kangaroo is licking saliva from its mother's mouth.

This is part of the mother-joey bonding process. It probably also helps the joey by passing on some of the tiny bacteria the young kangaroo will need to be able to digest plants.

While the young kangaroo continues to stay close to Mom and grow bigger, a new baby is born, crawls into the pouch, and starts to grow. The kangaroo family is definitely getting bigger—inside and outside Mom's pouch.

Clearly, kangaroos are special . . . from the inside out!

LOOKING BACK

1. Look at the size of the gray kangaroo's feet on the cover. When a kangaroo senses danger, it thumps its big feet to warn others. By the way, if you see a pouch, you will know the animal is a female. Only female kangaroos have pouches.

2. There is another way the musky rat kangaroo on page 5 is different than other kangaroos. It's the only kind of kangaroo to give birth to twins instead of just one baby at a time. Imagine how tiny those twins must be at birth!

3. Look closely at the red kangaroo digging on page 13. During a long dry period, kangaroos sometimes dig down as deep as a meter (3 feet) to find water. These "wells" also help other animals sharing the kangaroo's range.

4. On page 14, check out the eastern gray kangaroo's two big ears. Its large ears can be turned one at a time so one can be aimed forward and one backward. Even while it's resting, a kangaroo's ears are likely to be constantly moving as it listens for possible danger.

5. How many gray kangaroos can you count in the mob on page 16? Many farmers and ranchers think there are too many kangaroos. They view kangaroos as pests that knock down fences and use up the food and water they want for their sheep and cattle.

6. Take another look at page 17. Kangaroos come in all sizes. The biggest are just called kangaroos. Medium to small-sized kangaroos are called wallabies, like the Bennett's Wallaby. Even smaller are the rat kangaroos. The animals got their name when European explorers asked the native Australian people what these strange hopping animals were called. Their answer was "kangaroo," which means "I don't understand."

7. Take another look at the two males fighting on page 23. The largest male kangaroo in a mob usually wins out over smaller rivals. It's no wonder a male stands tall when it wants to impress an enemy. Male kangaroos have even been observed standing on tiptoe and balancing on their tails to look bigger.

8. Kangaroos are not silent. Most kangaroos make few noises, but they do grunt and cough. Red kangaroos make clicking sounds, and female grays like the one on page 32 cluck to call to their young.

GLOSSARY/INDEX

BACTERIA bak-tēr'-e-ə: Tiny living things that live in the kangaroo's body. They help break down plant cellulose and produce sugar and starch. Since they produce more than they can use, what is given off with their wastes is used by the kangaroo for food energy. The kangaroo also digests some of the bacteria to gain additional food nutrients. **20-21, 35**

BONES bōnz: The hard but lightweight parts that form the body's supporting frame. **9-10, 18**

BRAIN brān: Body part that receives messages about what is happening inside and outside the body and that sends messages to put the body into action. **22**

CARBON DIOXIDE kär'-b ə n dī-ok'-sīd: A gas that is given off naturally in body activities, carried to the lungs by the blood, and breathed out. **22, 26**

CELLS selz: Tiny building blocks for all body parts. **25**

EGG eg: Female reproductive cell. **25**

EMBRYO em'-brē-ō: Name given to the young developing in the womb. **25-26**

FAT fat: Food nutrient that supplies energy to live and grow. **30**

HEART härt: Body part that acts like a pump, constantly pushing blood throughout the kangaroo's body. **22**

JOEY jō'-ē: Name given to a baby kangaroo growing inside its mother's pouch. **25, 27-35**

LARGE INTESTINE lärj in-tes'-tin: Tube-shaped body part where bacteria attack still undigested plant material, supplying additional food nutrients. Wastes pass through the large intestine and out of the kangaroo's body. **21**

LUNG lə ng: Body part where oxygen and carbon dioxide are exchanged. **22**

MARSUPIAL mär-sü'-pē- əl: This is the scientific name given to the group of animals in which some of them have their young finish development inside a pouch. **3**

MOB mob: The name given to a group of kangaroos because they react to danger in a disorganized way, running in all directions. **16**

MUSCLES m ə s'- əlz: Working in pairs, muscles move the kangaroo's bones by pulling on them. **10**

NUTRIENTS nü'-trē- əntz: Chemical building blocks into which food is broken down for use by the kangaroo's body. The five basic nutrients provided by foods are proteins, fats, carbohydrates, minerals, and vitamins. **20-21, 22, 26, 30**

OXYGEN ok'-si-j ə n: A gas in the air that is breathed into the lungs, carried by the blood throughout the body, and combined with food nutrients to release energy. **22, 26**

PANT pant: Rapid passage of air into and out of the mouth. **14**

PROTEIN prō'-tēn: Nutrient needed by animal bodies to build tissues. **30**

SALIVA sə-lī'-və: Liquid produced in the mouth and licked onto the forearms to help regulate body heat in place of sweat. **15, 35**

SKELETON skel'-ə-tən: The framework of bones that supports the body and gives it its shape. **9**

SMALL INTESTINE sm äl in-tes'-tin: The tube-shaped body part where food is mixed with special digestive juices to break it down into nutrients. The nutrients then pass through the walls into the bloodstream. **21**

SPERM sp ərm: The male reproductive cell. **25**

STOMACH stəm'-ək: Tubelike body part where bacteria break down much of the plant material before it is passed into the small intestine. **20-21**

SWEAT swet: To produce a salty fluid that is given off through tiny openings in the skin. As sweat dries, heat is drawn away from the body for a cooling effect. Kangaroos only sweat when they are active. **15**

TENDON ten'-den: A stretchy band that connects muscles to bones. **7,10**

TONGUE tung: A movable muscle attached to the floor of the mouth. The kangaroo uses its tongue to shape the plants it is eating into a wad before swallowing. The kangaroo also uses its tongue to lick while grooming its coat or spreading saliva on its forearms. **14**

WINDPIPE wind'-pīp: Tube that carries air from the nose and mouth to the lungs and back out again. **22**

WOMB wüm: Female body part where the embryo develops before birth. **25**

ä as in c<u>a</u>rt   ā as in <u>**ape**</u>   ə as in b<u>a</u>nan<u>a</u>   ē as in <u>**e**</u>ven   ī as in b<u>**i**</u>te

ō as in g<u>**o**</u>   ü as in r<u>**u**</u>le   ʉ as in f<u>**ur**</u>

PHOTO CREDITS